If You Were A... Seed

Written by Claudia GJ Moore
Illustrated by Alex Garcia

First Published in 2024 by Blossom Spring Publishing
If You Were A… Seed Copyright © 2024 Claudia GJ Moore
ISBN 978-1-7385023-7-0
E: admin@blossomspringpublishing.com
W: www.blossomspringpublishing.com
Claudia GJ Moore as the author and Alex Garcia as the illustrator,
have been asserted in accordance with the Copyright, Designs and Patents Act,1988.
All rights reserved under International Copyright Law.
Contents and/or cover may not be reproduced in whole or in part without the
express written consent of the publisher.

"With boundless love to my family, who are my sturdy ground, my warm sunlight and my happy raindrops. ILUTM, Claudia.

To B. Alex."

If you were a... seed

Would you settle in a pot?
Would you settle by a road?
Would you settle in a meadow?
Would you settle by your school's front door?

If you were to settle in a pot...
You could grow.
You could grow with a kind and daily greeting.

You could receive a frequent and refreshing drop
And a manicured trimming.
You could surely grow.

And if you do…

You would look your best and, in that pot, you would dress up
a windowsill, a corridor, an entrance, a home.
You would be praised and adored.
Devoted hands and loving eyes will make you proud.
**What a happy existence if you were a seed
and settled in a pot!**

But if you were to settle by a road…

You could grow.
You could grow despite the dangers and the noise.
You would not be tended to daily or loved.
Instead, you would grow mighty and strong.
The occasional hello and the erratic rain would make you bond with all the rest.
You could have buzzing bees and other dainty insects as your friends. You could surely grow.

And if you do…

Resilience would be your strength.
What a mighty existence if you were a seed and settled by a road!

But if you were to settle in a meadow…

You could grow.
You could grow amongst a hundred million others.
There would be, of course, the elements to be weary of and worried, but together you could create a scene of wonders.
You could surely grow.

And if you do...

You would be part of a paradise for spindly bugs
and wriggly flutters,
For tiny creatures and all sorts of bold explorers.
Carefree and jolly, a vast wilderness the meadow
life would promise.
**What an exciting and free existence if you were a seed
and settled in a meadow!**

But if you were to settle by your school's front door...
You could grow.
You could grow and in others kindle amazement and awe.
The curious minds of your five-day week audience would wonder and eventually draw
Your vivid colour, whether bumblebee yellows, berry blues, apple reds or green sheen forests.
You could surely grow.

And if you do...

You would inspire and become the sparkle of brilliant ideas, the warmest.
Your days will be filled with giggles, a splendid children's choir and everyone's future desires.
What an amazing existence if you were a seed and settled by your school's front door!

But no matter where you settle, If you were a seed,

You ought to grow due to the
Goodness of the planet's rich soil.

The beaming of the faraway sun.

The softness of the everlasting rainfall.

These will enable you to sprout a root and help you to emerge into this world,
To provide and to provoke,
To inspire and to absorb.

So, next time you find yourself a little seed,
think of all the possibilities and life that lies within.

Because, what if you were a...

seed.

Glossary

Seed

The baby of a plant intended to become like the parent-plant if all conditions are met adequately (nutritious soil, beaming sun and refreshing rain.)

Most plants produce seeds by which they reproduce, survive and thrive.

Some seeds sleep through winter inside bulbs. For example, daffodils and tulips.

Seeds can be super tiny, like mustard seeds. Or very, very big and heavy, like coconut seeds. All seeds need to find their own space, light and water to thrive.

One of the many successes of plants on our planet is the way in which seeds are spread and how they cleverly travel to find their own space.

Seeds can be carried by the wind, by animals, by water and by humans, just like you and me!

Seed dispersal

Examples of wind dispersal seeds:
milkweed, dandelion, maple.

Examples of seeds dispersed by animals:
beggar-ticks, sandbur, blackberry.

Examples of seeds dispersed by water:
lotus, cattail, coconut.

Examples of seeds dispersed by humans:
bean, wheat, cherry.

Seeds and the fruit that contain them are a very good source of food for many living creatures.

Can you think of any seeds you like to eat?

Can you think of the shape of seeds in your favourite plant, fruit or vegetable?

Have a go at drawing your favourite seed!

Remember that plants produce the oxygen we need to breathe.
So, please look after all the plants, the trees and, if you can, plant a seed and help it to grow and thrive.
Because, how magical to be a seed!

About The Author

Born in Mexico City, Claudia is a keen traveller and a passionate educator. She began her career in teaching soon after becoming a mother.

In the summer of 2015, while living in a charming old village house in the south of England, her decade-long idea of writing children's books started to take shape and the idea of stepping into someone or something else's journey through life, started to emerge.

As an educator, she has always tried to push the boundaries of language and imagination by providing exciting, ambitious vocabulary and ideas to children - as she believes there's no better age to do so. She hopes to tap into children's wondrous creativity and provide a way for parents, teachers and carers to rocket children's imaginations with the beautiful world of words.

About The Illustrator

Alex Garcia began his artistic career at a young age. A playwright, director and actor in his early twenties, he produced thought-provoking theatre in Mexico City.

Alex is a self-taught painter who began experimenting with watercolours a decade ago. He had his first watercolour exhibition in 2018 at V&S Gallery in the city of Mexico, where many of his pieces were highly sought after.
Alex has stepped out of his comfort zone with rigour and enthusiasm as an illustrator for the first time with this book. How happy we are that he has risen to the challenge!

Alex lives in Mexico City with his beautiful wife, Anabeli, where he teaches English Language at University and paints for pleasure in his spare time.

www.blossomspringpublishing.com

www.ingramcontent.com/pod-product-compliance
Lightning Source LLC
Chambersburg PA
CBHW041541040426
42446CB00002B/180